Roobarb

Roobarb & Custard

Meet the gang!

Custard

Mouse

Moggy
Malone

Mole

When Roobarb found the hieroglyphics

First published in Great Britain 2009 by Mogzilla Ltd. No part of this publication may be reproduced, stored in a retrieval system, or transmitted in any form or by any means electronic, mechanical, photocopying, recording or otherwise without the prior permission of the publisher and copyright owner. This book is sold subject to the condition that it shall not be leant, re-sold, hired-out or otherwise circulated without the publisher and copyright owner's prior consent, in any form of binding or cover other than that in which it is published and without a similar condition, including this condition being imposed on the subsequent publisher.

www.roobarbandcustard.tv © 1974-2009 A&B TV limited. All rights reserved. Roobarb & Custard created by Grange Calveley.

© Mogzilla 2009 www.mogzilla.co.uk/roobarbandcustard ISBN: 978-1-906132-18-7. Printed in Malta. 5 4 3 2 1 -

It was a very still day.

The clouds didn't move. The birds didn't move.

It was a very still day indeed!

Roobarb decided to spend the day treasure hunting.

Suddenly, Roobarb spied something shiny in the grass.
Before he could pick it up, a muddy hand grabbed it.

'Grrrrr!' growled Roobarb, jumping up and down in anger, waking up Custard.

'I found some treasure on the lawn. But now it's gone!' moaned Roobarb, and feeling miserable, he sloped off to his shed.

In the shed, a trapdoor opened and out popped Mole.

'Somebody's swiped my treasure!'

howled Roobarb.

'Don't worry, boyo,'

muttered Mole,

'I'll help you get it back.'

Roobarb followed his Welsh friend through the trapdoor.

On the other side was a huge cave with steps leading

down,

down,

down.

They came to an enormous room, stuffed full of treasure.

Diamonds

Gold coins

Egyptian stuff

Even pictures of
ancient bus queues.

'Where did you find all this?'
asked Roobarb curiously.

'I'll open a marvellous museum!' mused Roobarb, 'I know what I need!'

He dashed back to the shed for his tools.

'He's been thundering up and down that garden for hours and he's not found a sausage,' Mole mumbled. 'I'd better help him out.'

A few minutes later, Roobarb found one of the coins that Mole had hidden.

'It's treasure!'

shouted Roobarb.

'An Egyptian cat!' roared Roobarb excitedly,
'The reclining one will enjoy this!'

As Roobarb polished the gold coin, something strange happened...

The ground *trembled* and the sky went dark.

Suddenly, a giant cat appeared.
'I am Mee-Ow, the God-cat of ancient Egypt,' it purred.
When it saw Custard, it smiled.

'I, Mee-Ow, grant a wish to the miserable one known as Custard. Speak, pink one,' said the giant cat.
Custard looked up t r e m b l i n g.

'Er,' he mumbled. 'I wish for a gold...' but before Custard could finish, gold coins and all manner of shiny treasure began to fall from the sky!

Trying to avoid the shower of falling coins, Roobarb said in his best Custard voice:

'I wish all this gold would go away!'

With a crash of thunder, Mee-Ow vanished and the gold stopped falling.

'Thank heavens for that!' said Roobarb.

'Oi, boyo!'

came the voice of Mole,

'All my gold has disappeared!'

'Oh dear,'

said Roobarb.

It was a very still day.

Bag yourself more Roobarb & Custard books online at
www.mogzilla.co.uk/shop

'The gentle wit and charm of these new Roobarb stories will delight toddlers and parents. Young children will love the chaos that ensues not just between the forever joking Roobarb, the green dog and the wacky pink cat, Custard but with the rest of their gang too...it's guaranteed to be laugh-out-loud funny. Great for parents to read aloud with their children.'

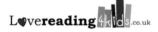

'...faithfully crammed with all the slapstick and layers of subtler humour you'd expect. Simultaneously nostalgic and fresh, they're bound to please those who remember this green and pink pair from the first time around, as well as a new generation of fans.'

Teach Primary Magazine

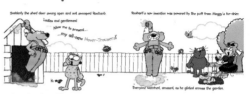

When Roobarb's trousers flew
ISBN: 978-1-906132-14-9 (Large format)

When Roobarb found the hieroglyphics
ISBN: 978-1-906132-11-8 (Large format)

When Custard was grounded
ISBN: 978-1-906132-10-1 (Large format)

When there was a pottery party
ISBN: 978-1-906132-12-5 (Large format)

When there was a ballet
ISBN: 978-1-906132-13-2 (Large format)

Roobarb & Custard in your pocket!

When there was a pottery party
ISBN: 978-1-906132-1-94
Pocket-size

When there was a ballet
ISBN: 978-1-906132-2-00
Pocket-size

When Custard was grounded
ISBN: 978-1-906132-17-0
Pocket-size

You can order any of these fab little titles from www.mogzilla.co.uk